Jonathan Clarkson Gibbs

Reconstruction Revolutionary

Stephanie Paris

Consultants

Dorothy Levin, M.S.Ed., MBA
St. Lucie County Schools

Vanessa Ann Gunther, Ph.D.
Department of History
Chapman University

Cassandra Slone
Pinellas County Public Schools

Publishing Credits

Rachelle Cracchiolo, M.S.Ed., *Publisher*
Conni Medina, M.A.Ed., *Managing Editor*
Emily R. Smith, MA.Ed., *Series Developer*
Diana Kenney, M.A.Ed., NBCT, *Content Director*
Courtney Patterson, *Multimedia Designer*

Image Credits: Cover and pp.1, 2-3, 4, 18, 20, 22, 22-23, 24, 26, 29 (bottom), 31 State Archives of Florida; cover, pp.1, 13, 28 Creative Commons Troy, New York by Doug Kerr used under CC BY-SA 2.0; p.5 Dayton Metro Library Map Collection; pp.6, 9, 21 North Wind Picture Archives; p.7 LOC [g3820.rr002900]; p.8 LOC [LC-USZ62-68464]; pp.11, 27 Courtesy of Dartmouth College Library; p.14 (right) Wikimedia Commons/Public Domain; p.15 Chronicle/Alamy, (top) LOC [lprbscsm.scsm0921]; pp.16, 17, 29 (middle) Granger, NYC; p.19 (top) State Archives of Florida/Slade, (bottom) LOC [LC-USZC4-5342]; p.25 (right) To Davie Jeems Ku Klux Klan, Circa 1868 (Courtesy of The Gilder Lehrman Institute of American History, GLC09090), (left) New York Public Library Digital Collections; pp.26, back cover Photo courtesy of Stewart Signs; p.29 (top) LOC [LC-USZ62-68464]; p.32 LOC [LC-USZC4-5342]; all other images from iStock and/or Shutterstock.

Library of Congress Cataloging-in-Publication Data

Names: Paris, Stephanie Herweck, author.
Title: Jonathan Clarkson Gibbs : Reconstruction revolutionary / Stephanie
Paris.
Description: Huntington Beach, CA : Teacher Created Materials, 2016. |
Includes index. | Audience: Grade 4 to 6.
Identifiers: LCCN 2016014354 (print) | LCCN 2016015182 (ebook) | ISBN
9781493835409 (pbk.) | ISBN 9781480756380 (eBook)
Subjects: LCSH: Gibbs, Jonathan C. (Jonathan Clarkson), 1831-1874--Juvenile
literature. | African Americans--Florida--Biography--Juvenile literature.
| Florida. Office of Secretary of State--Biography--Juvenile literature. |
Florida. Department of Public Instruction--Biography--Juvenile literature.
| Reconstruction (U.S. history, 1865-1877)--Florida--Juvenile literature.
| Florida--History--1865---Juvenile literature. |
Florida--Biography--Juvenile literature.
Classification: LCC F316.G53 P37 2016 (print) | LCC F316.G53 (ebook) | DDC
975.9/06092 [B] --dc23
LC record available at https://lccn.loc.gov/2016014354

Teacher Created Materials
5301 Oceanus Drive
Huntington Beach, CA 92649-1030
http://www.tcmpub.com

ISBN 978-1-4938-3540-9

Made in China
Nordica.082016.CA21601381

Table of Contents

Part of the Change

The 1800s were a time of great change in the United States. Slavery was a **ghastly** truth for many. Luckily, there were people who worked to change this unjust system. They used the skills and resources they had to do so. Some of them sheltered runaway slaves in the **Underground Railroad**. Some fought to change laws. Others gave clothes and shelter to freed slaves.

Jonathan Clarkson Gibbs was someone who wanted to be a part of the change. He was **charismatic**. He could speak well. He could convince people to listen to what he had to say and take action. He was also very smart. The things he had to say made sense to people. He used these gifts to become a minister. He then became a politician and an educator. He used all of his jobs to make a difference in the lives of people in his time and beyond.

Underground Railroad

The Underground Railroad was not a train. It was a network of people and safe houses that helped slaves escape to free states and other countries.

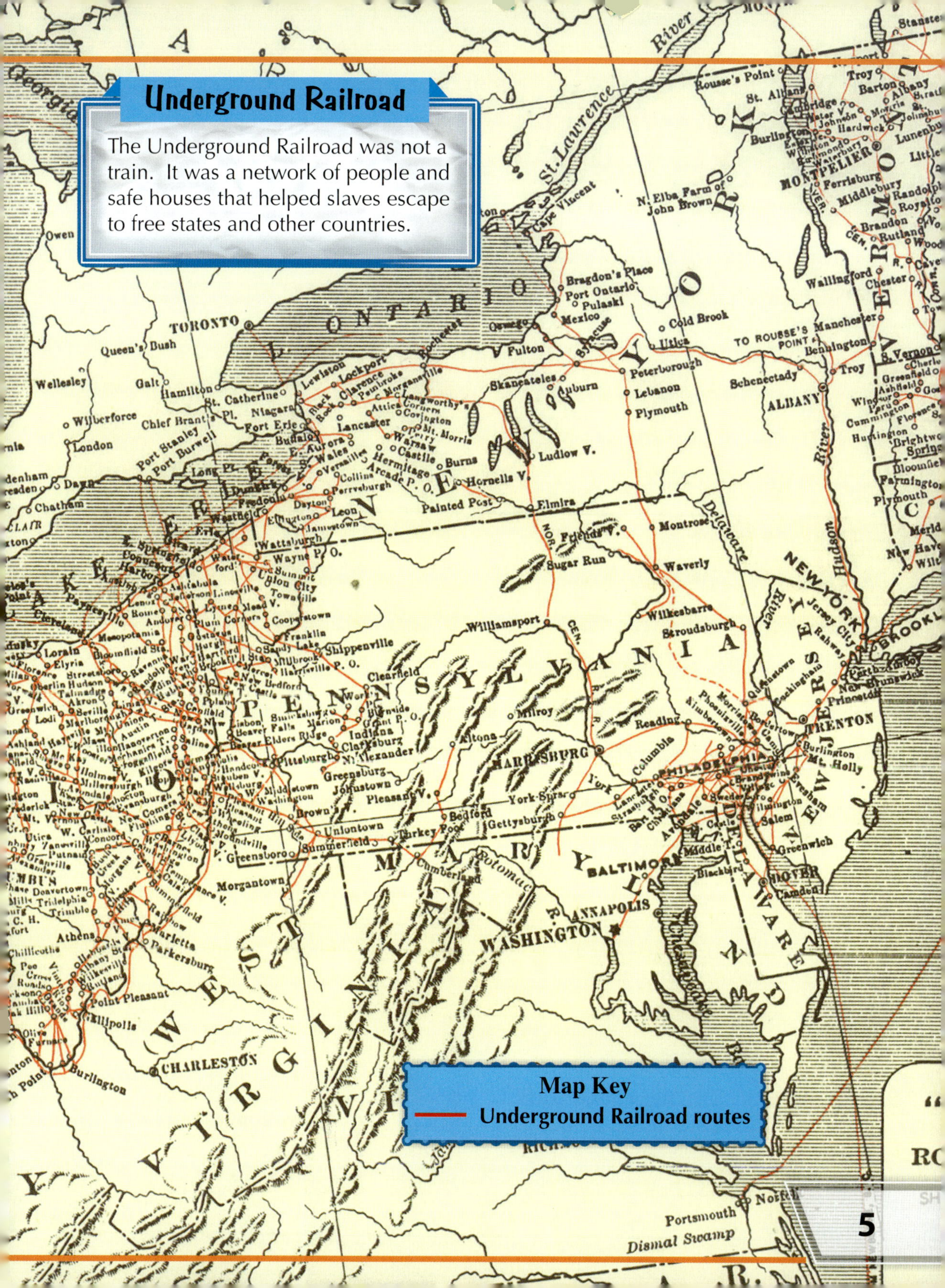

A Challenging Childhood

Jonathan Clarkson Gibbs II was born in the 1820s. His family lived in Philadelphia, Pennsylvania. The state had largely ended slavery, so Gibbs was born free. But that did not mean life was easy. There was a lot of conflict. Many people did not want change. They did not think everyone should have the same rights. Sometimes people were violent. Anti-black riots were common.

Philadelphia in the 1800s

The Gibbs family had three more children. The family was never well off. His father, Jonathan Gibbs, was a minister. Ministers did not make a lot of money. Life got harder in 1831 when Gibbs's father died suddenly. Gibbs's mother, Maria, struggled to support the family on her own. She took in laundry. But the work and the stress were too much. She could not work enough to keep everyone fed. Soon, she got sick. With her illness, they became frantic. Something had to change or they would starve.

Date of Birth

Jonathan Clarkson Gibbs was either born on September 28, 1821; October 21, 1821; October 28, 1828; or "sometime in 1827." Existing records have conflicting dates.

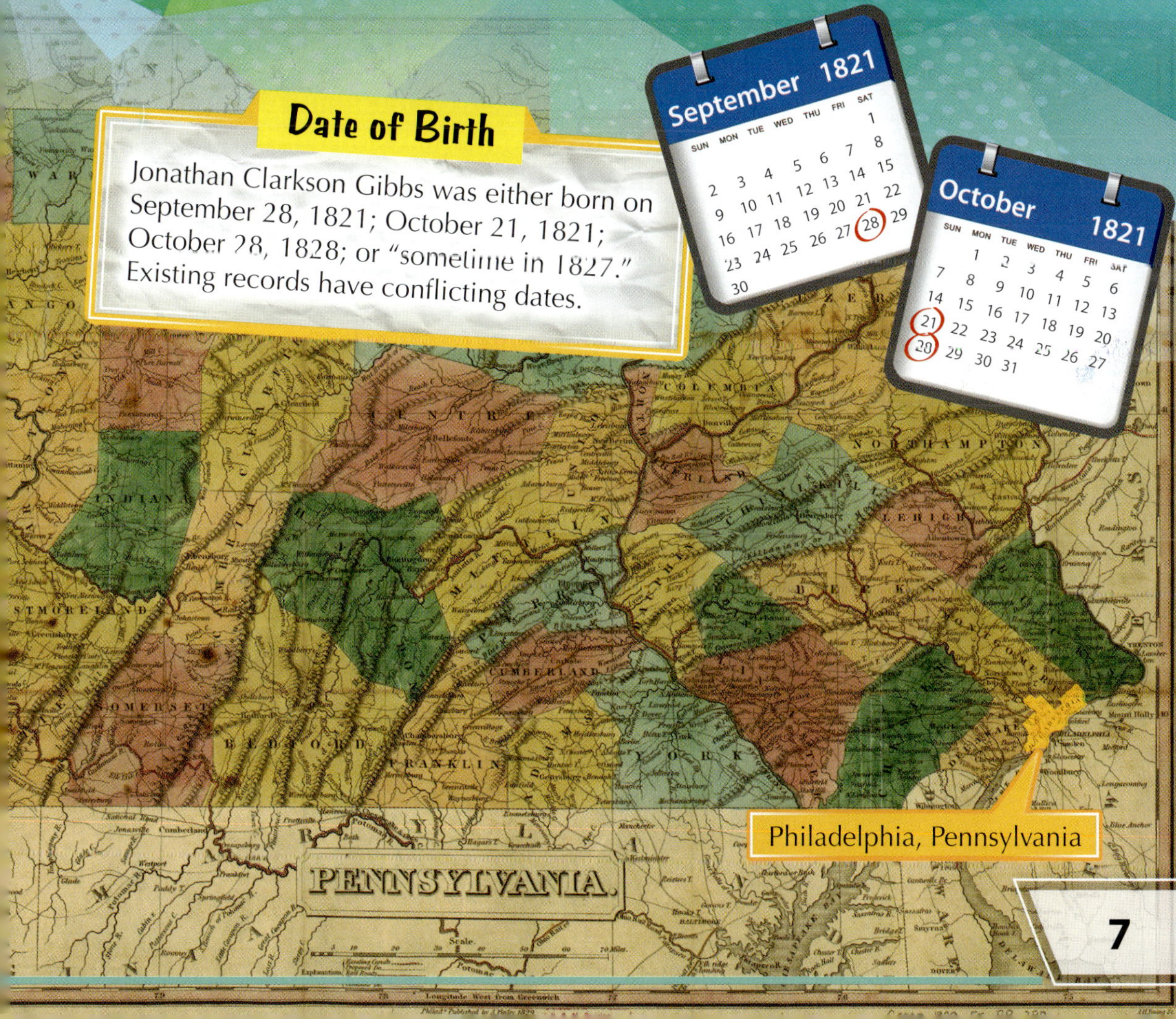

Temporary Setbacks

Jonathan Gibbs and his younger brother, Mifflin, had been going to school. But now the family needed money. There were no organizations to help the family. The brothers had to quit school. They had to find jobs to provide for the family. Gibbs was around 12 when they left school to work. But that was only a brief setback as far as he was concerned. They had to help their family in its time of need.

There was a well-known black carpenter in town named James Gibbons. The boys asked him for work. He understood their situation. He also saw that they were willing to learn. So, he hired them. They started working as **apprentice** carpenters. The money helped the family. They were still poor, but now they could eat regularly. Still, Gibbs missed school. There weren't many options for a young black man during this time. So, Gibbs started thinking of ways he and his brother could get an education.

The school Gibbs went to might have looked similar to this one.

A carpenter's apprentice smooths and shapes wood in the 1800s.

Seeking Education

Their first plan was to find a new church. They joined the First African Presbyterian Church of Philadelphia. Being the sons of a minister had taught them that churches could be strong community centers. The leaders at their new church helped educate people. They also organized political groups. Gibbs impressed the church leaders so much that they offered to pay for his education. They sent him to the Kimball Union Academy (KUA). When he was done, Gibbs wanted to learn more. Nearby was a well-known school called Dartmouth College.

A man named Dr. Nathan Lord ran Dartmouth. Lord was a deep thinker. He was also very religious. He was known for doing things differently than most people. Gibbs applied to Dartmouth. He also applied to 18 other colleges. At the time, most of the schools only took white students. All of the other schools turned Gibbs down. But, Dr. Lord accepted him.

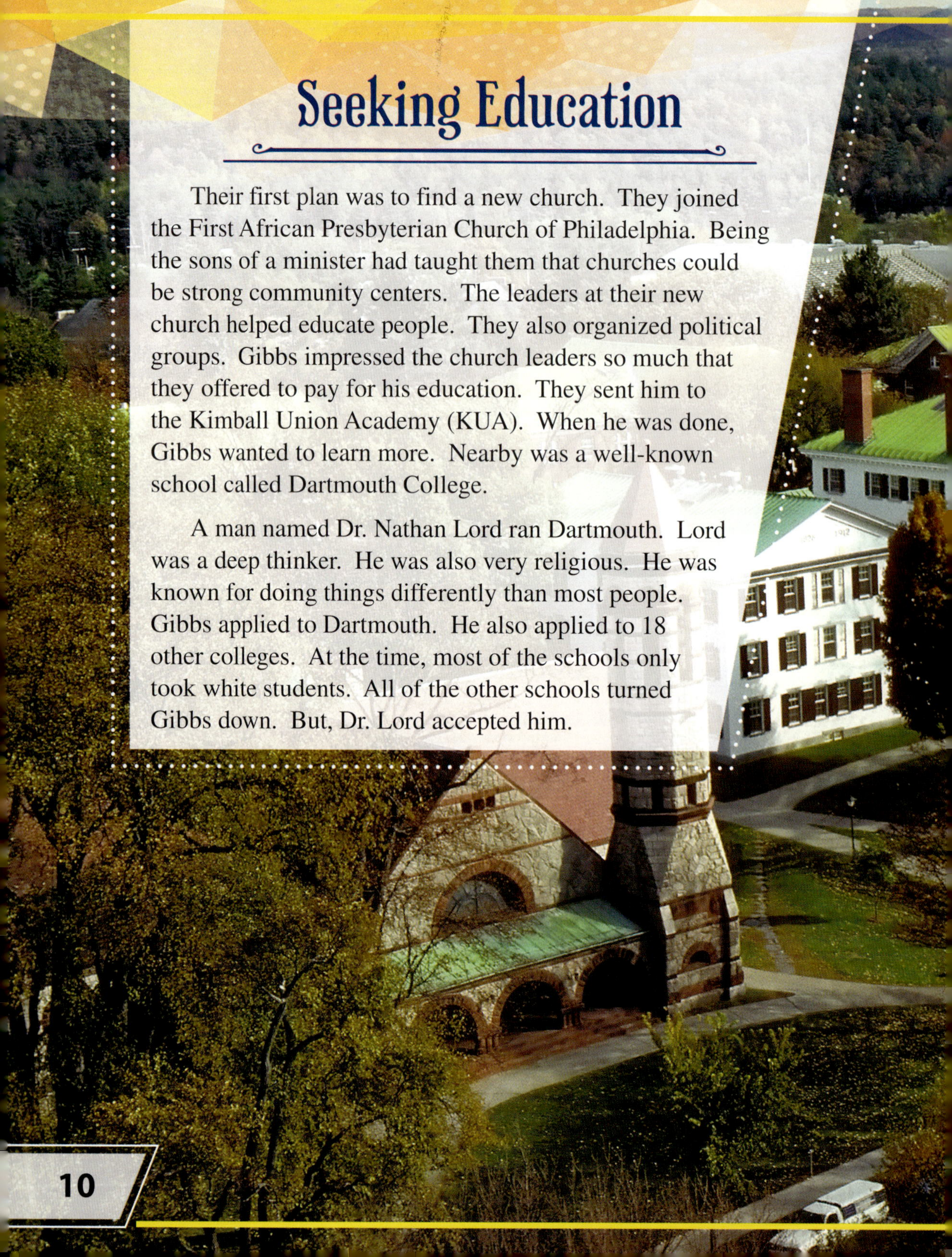

Dartmouth today

Pro-Education

At the time that Gibbs applied, Dr. Lord was pro-slavery. He thought the Bible supported it. But, he thought that everyone should have the opportunity to learn.

Dr. Nathan Lord

Gibbs studied with many bold thinkers. He found himself getting more politically active. He started working to end slavery.

Gibbs finished his time at Dartmouth in 1852. He was the second African American in history to give a graduation speech at an American college. His speech was called "The Egyptian Obelisk in the Court of St. Peter."

Gibbs wasn't done, though. He was ready to take his next step. He entered a **seminary**. Even though he never graduated, he was **ordained** as a minister four years later.

Gibbs soon became a pastor in Troy, New York. His church was called Liberty Street Presbyterian Church. He married his first wife, Anna Amelia Harris, around this time. She was the daughter of a successful businessman. The couple had two children.

One of the First

Gibbs was only the third known black graduate of Dartmouth College. He studied Latin, Greek, math, morals, and philosophy.

Gibbs was a pastor at a church like this one.

An Active Career

Gibbs used his role as a pastor to help spread his message. His sermons echoed the ideas of the **abolitionist** movement. He spoke about the rights people should have. He wrote about the need for change in the country. Gibbs became a well-known speaker and activist.

Gibbs's career kept him very busy. He worked with abolitionists, such as Frederick Douglass and Martin Delaney. He campaigned for voting rights. He protested to end **segregation** on New York City streetcars. And, he traveled a lot to do these things. This caused problems in his marriage over time. His wife left him in 1857. She gave birth to their third child shortly after. In 1862, Gibbs and his wife divorced.

Frederick Douglass

Martin Delaney

By this time, Gibbs had moved back to Philadelphia. He became the pastor of the same church that had sent him to KUA. On January 1, 1863, President Lincoln issued the Emancipation Proclamation. It gave all slaves in the rebellious states their freedom. It was a step in the right direction. Gibbs gave a sermon called "Freedom's Joyful Day" to mark the special day. He praised people who had fought for this freedom. He rejoiced at the chance to fight alongside white soldiers in the **Civil War**.

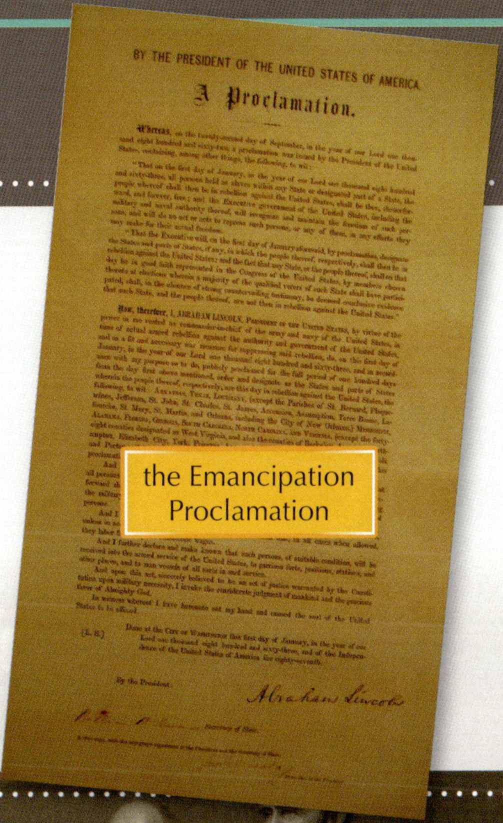
BY THE PRESIDENT OF THE UNITED STATES OF AMERICA

A Proclamation.

the Emancipation Proclamation

Lincoln and his cabinet members read the Emancipation Proclamation for the first time.

A Union soldier poses with African Americans on a plantation in South Carolina in 1862.

Reconstructing the Country

In 1865, Jonathan Gibbs headed south to help the **freedmen**. He went to both North and South Carolina. He wanted to help the former slaves and others who were left with nothing after the war. This period of rebuilding was called **Reconstruction**.

Black Codes

Many Southern states passed laws after the Civil War called black codes. The laws limited the things former slaves could and could not do. When the U.S. government made black codes illegal, states passed Jim Crow laws. These laws kept black and white people separate.

This 1867 illustration depicts a black veteran arguing for his right to vote.

Freedmen's School in South Carolina

About this time, Gibbs met and married his second wife, Elizabeth. They had a daughter named Anne.

Gibbs's career continued to keep him busy. He started a school so freedmen could learn to read and write. He held events that encouraged people to ask for more rights.

Sadly, all his work wasn't welcomed. The white community saw him as an outsider coming in to cause trouble. The local church sent him to a smaller town where he would cause less of a disturbance. Gibbs was not happy.

Eventually, Gibbs moved to Florida. There, he separated himself from the church. But he continued to serve in a different way. He devoted more of his time to politics.

Gibbs quickly gained political attention. His politics were fairly extreme for his time. He thought about joining an equally extreme group of the Republican Party. But, he joined a middle-of-the-road group instead. He thought he could get more support that way. His choice paid off. He was chosen to be part of the group that would write the new constitution for Florida.

Gibbs pressed for African Americans to have more rights in the state. Others wanted to give more power to the defeated Confederate **rebels**. There were compromises in the end. The document gave black men the right to vote. It made public education free, too.

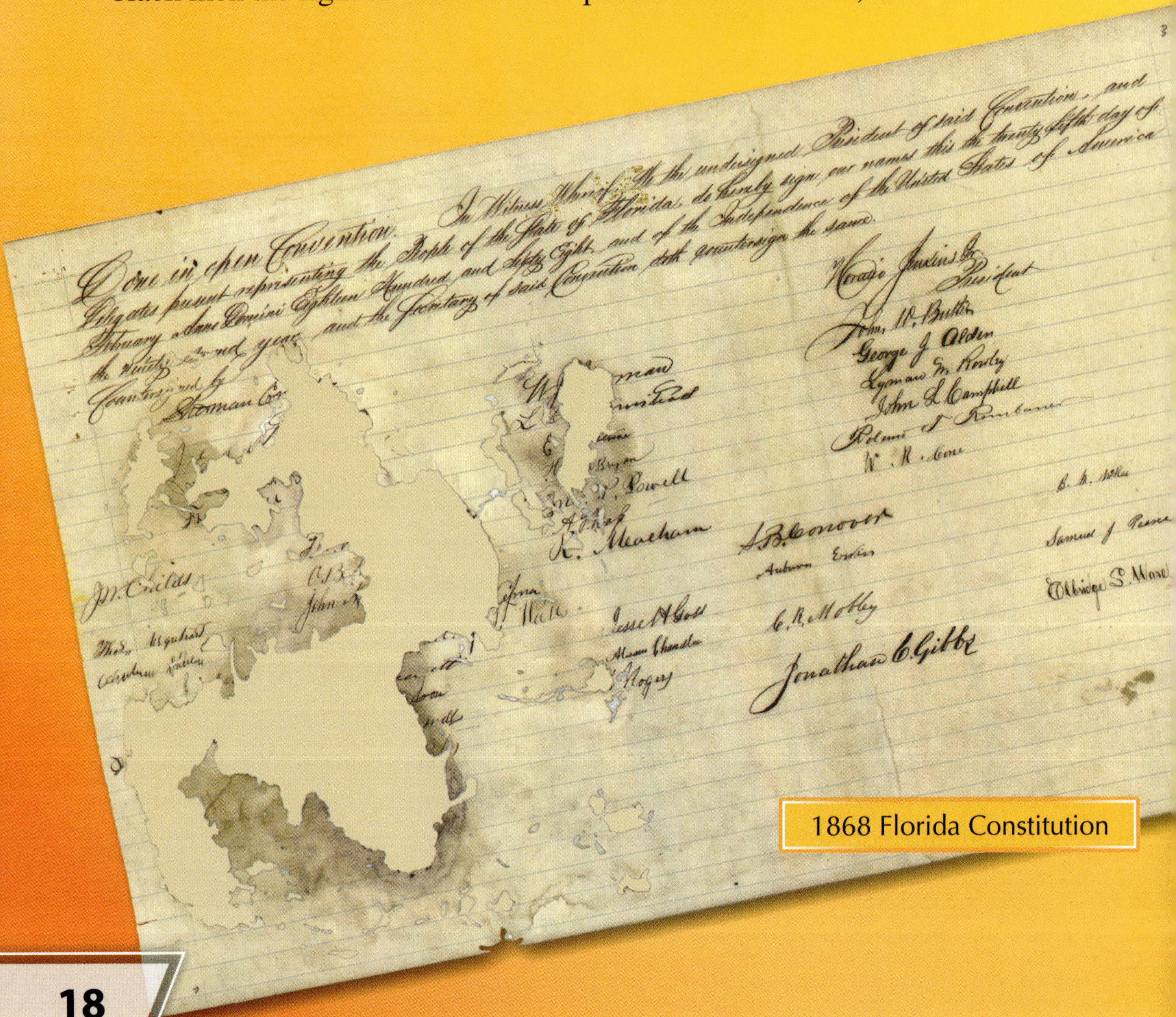

1868 Florida Constitution

By now, Harrison Reed had become the new **governor** of Florida. Reed was impressed with Gibbs's work as a delegate. In 1868, Reed offered him a new job. The job was **secretary of state** of Florida.

Harrison Reed

Political Ads

This 1866 political ad illustrates the racist opinions of the time. Democrats opposed the expansion of voting rights. Republicans supported the expansion.

Secretary of State

Gibbs became the first black secretary of state of Florida in 1868. The job gave him a lot of power. In fact, when the governor was away, Gibbs sometimes served as acting governor. He used his power to push for more rights and better treatment of freed slaves. He investigated violence that had occurred. He looked into fraud. He helped maintain order when people tried to **impeach** the governor.

Impeachment

Some people didn't agree with Harrison Reed's political views. They were afraid that he would give too much power to black politicians. They wanted him to be removed from office. However, Reed was not impeached because proper procedures had not taken place.

Florida's Capitol Building in the 1800s

Gibbs also investigated the actions of a group called the Ku Klux Klan. This group did not want African Americans to have more rights. The Klan and others threatened Gibbs. Some sources say that the Klan even tried to kill Gibbs in 1870. But Gibbs did not let that stop him. He kept trying to make things better in the state for all people.

Members of the Ku Klux Klan threaten a man.

Ossian B. Hart

Superintendent of Public Instruction

The next governor elected in Florida was Ossian B. Hart. In 1873, he asked Gibbs to take a new job. Gibbs became the first black **superintendent of public instruction** of Florida. By all accounts, this was an excellent fit for Gibbs.

Florida schools were suffering from many problems. They didn't have enough teachers. They didn't have suitable buildings. And they didn't have enough money. Gibbs worked to improve education for all students. He insisted that school leaders give him regular reports about progress. He required schools to use the same textbooks. He insisted they teach the same topics. He tried to find money to fund two schools for ex-slaves. He tried to fight laws that prevented black and white students from attending the same schools. Gibbs worked to make education better in the state.

Union Academy in Gainesville, Florida

A Mysterious Death

On August 14, 1874, Gibbs spoke to a group of local Republicans. Hours after returning home, he was found dead. The official cause of death was apoplexy (AP-uh-plek-see), or a stroke. But many people have another theory about his death.

Final Photo

This was one of the last pictures taken of Gibbs in 1874. Florida Governor Marcellus Stearns and his cabinet stand on the steps of the Capitol Building with Harriet Beecher Stowe. Gibbs poses by one of the columns.

Some people believe that the Ku Klux Klan poisoned him. A few months earlier, the Klan had threatened Gibbs. Gibbs was a high-profile target because he was so vocal. The group did not like him. So in response to the Klan's threats, Gibbs kept himself armed. He wanted to protect himself and his family. Sometimes he even slept in the attic of his house to hide from potential intruders. For these reasons, many people claim he was murdered.

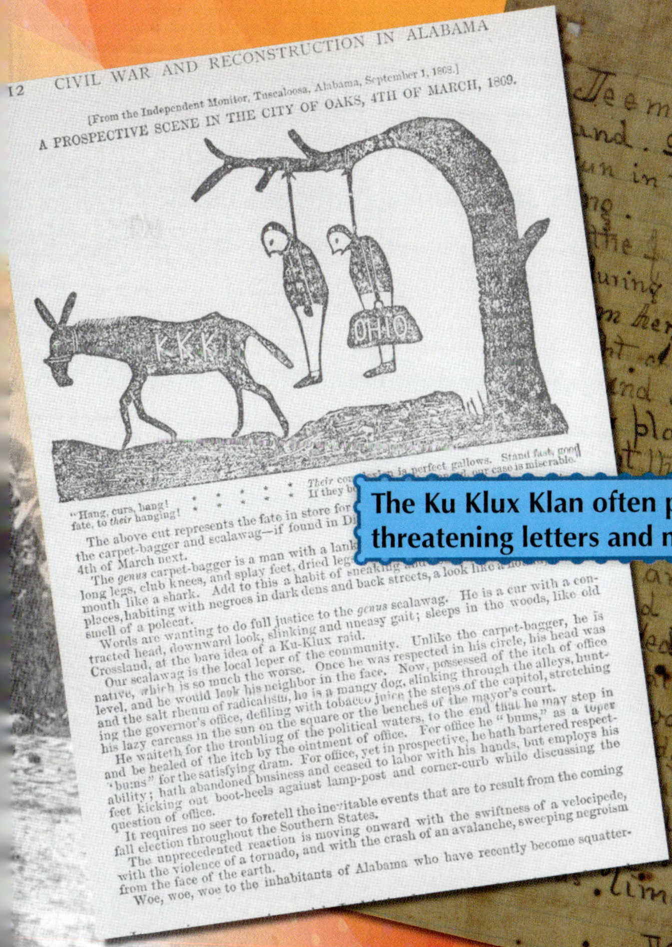

12 CIVIL WAR AND RECONSTRUCTION IN ALABAMA

[From the Independent Monitor, Tuscaloosa, Alabama, September 1, 1868.]

A PROSPECTIVE SCENE IN THE CITY OF OAKS, 4TH OF MARCH, 1869.

"Hang, curs, hang! * * * * * *Their* com[illegible] is perfect gallows. Stand fast, good fate, to *their* hanging! * * * * * If they b[illegible] our case is miserable."

The above cut represents the fate in store for the carpet-bagger and scalawag—if found in Di[illegible] 4th of March next.

The *genus* carpet-bagger is a man with a lank[illegible] long legs, club knees, and splay feet, dried leg[illegible] mouth like a shark. Add to this a habit of sneaking [illegible] places, habiting with negroes in dark dens and back streets, a look like a [illegible] smell of a polecat.

Words are wanting to do full justice to the *genus* scalawag. He is a cur with a contracted head, downward look, slinking and uneasy gait; sleeps in the woods, like old Crossland, at the bare idea of a Ku-Klux raid.

Our scalawag is the local leper of the community. Unlike the carpet-bagger, he is native, *which* is so much the worse. Once he was respected in his circle, his head was level, and he would look his neighbor in the face. Now, possessed of the itch of office and the salt rheum of radicalism, he is a mangy dog, slinking through the alleys, hunting the governor's office, defiling with tobacco juice the steps of the capitol, stretching his lazy carcass in the sun on the square or the benches of the mayor's court.

He waiteth for the troubling of the political waters, to the end that he may step in and be healed of the itch by the ointment of office. For office he "bums," as a toper "bums" for the satisfying dram. For office, yet in prospective, he hath bartered respectability; hath abandoned business and ceased to labor with his hands, but employs his feet kicking out boot-heels against lamp-post and corner-curb while discussing the question of office.

It requires no seer to foretell the inevitable events that are to result from the coming fall election throughout the Southern States.

The unprecedented reaction is moving onward with the swiftness of a velocipede, with the violence of a tornado, and with the crash of an avalanche, sweeping negroism from the face of the earth.

Woe, woe, woe to the inhabitants of Alabama who have recently become squatter-

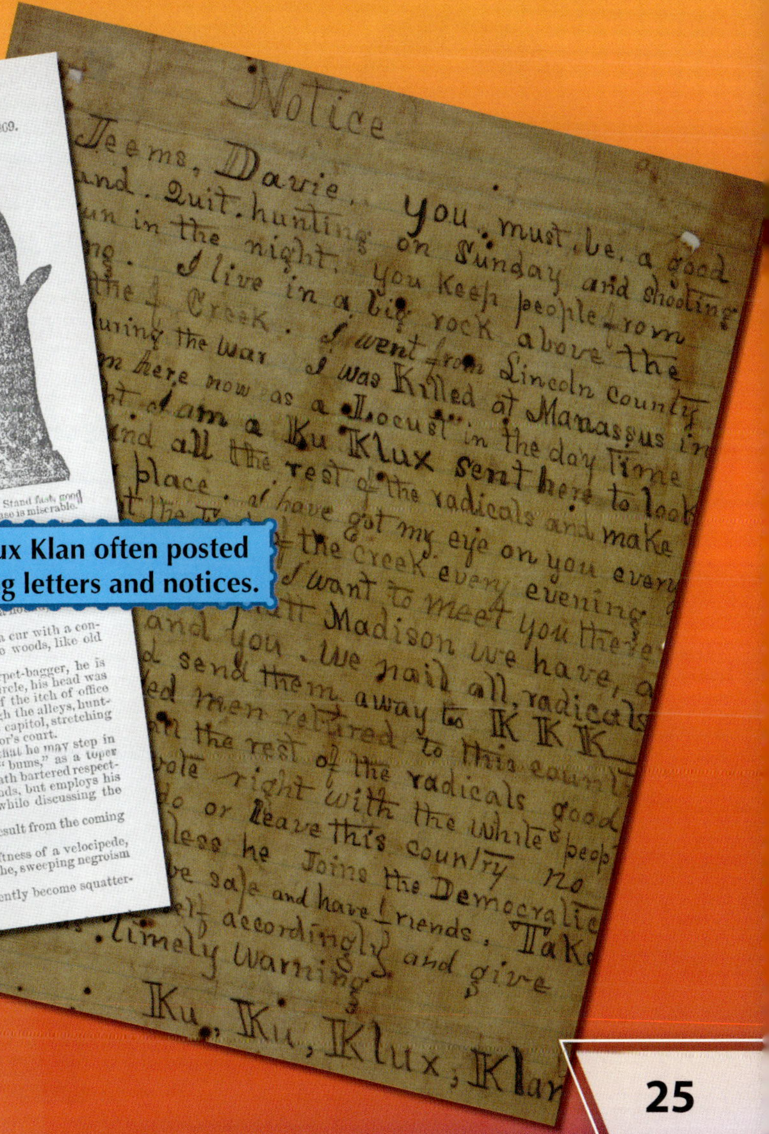

Notice

Jeems, Davie. you must be a good
and. Quit hunting on Sunday and shooting
un in the night. you keep people from
ng. I live in a big rock above the
the Creek. I went from Lincoln County
uring the war I was Killed at Manassus in
m here now as a Locust in the day Time
t. I am a Ku Klux sent here to look
nd all the rest of the radicals and make
place. I have got my eye on you every
t the [illegible] of the Creek every evening
I want to meet you there
and [illegible] Madison we have, a
and you. we nail all radicals
d send them away to K K K
ed men returned to this county
n the rest of the radicals good
vote right with the white peop
do or leave this country no
less he Joins the Democratic
be safe and have friends. Take
[illegible] accordingly and give
. timely warning
Ku, Ku, Klux, Klan

The Ku Klux Klan often posted threatening letters and notices.

Education and Equality

Jonathan Clarkson Gibbs started life under challenging circumstances. The death of his father could have stopped him. The need to leave school could have stopped him. The conflicts he encountered throughout adulthood could have stopped him. Yet, he persevered. He was smart. He looked for opportunities. He worked toward his goals at all times. Many of his achievements can be measured in firsts, seconds, and thirds. He was the first black secretary of state of Florida. He was the first black superintendent of public instruction of Florida. He was the second black man to give a graduation speech at an American college. He was the third black man to graduate from Dartmouth. The list goes on.

Jonathan Clarkson Gibbs

Gibbs was a revolutionary. He laid the path for many men and women to follow. He worked bravely with that very goal in mind. He refused to let threats or unfair policies stand in his way. Jonathan Clarkson Gibbs made a difference.

In His Honor

Gibbs was an influential person in Florida. People wanted to remember all that he did. Gibbs High School in St. Petersburg is named after him.

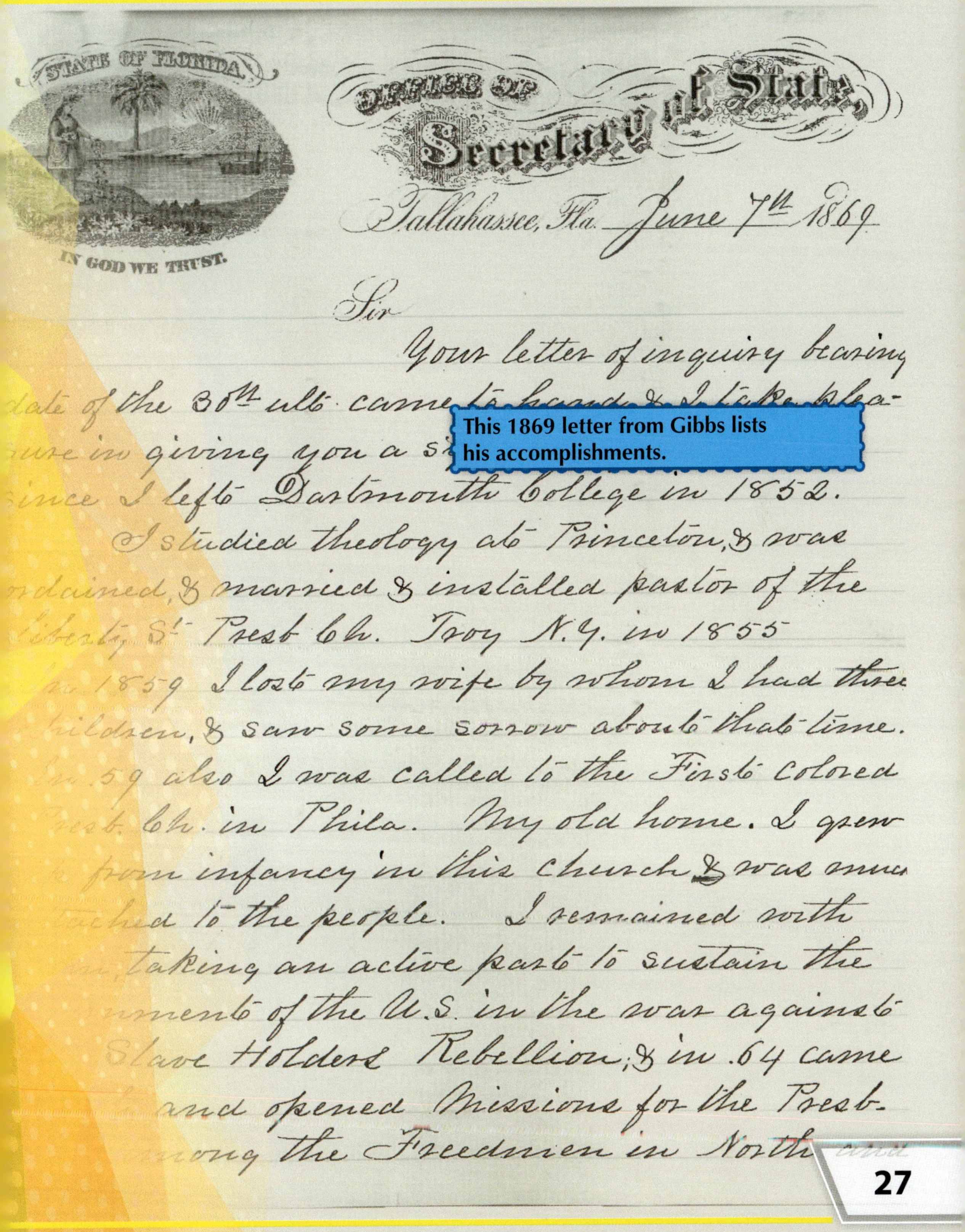

Sir

Your letter of inquiry bearing date of the 30th ult. came to hand & I take plea-sure in giving you a s[illegible] since I left Dartmouth College in 1852.

I studied theology at Princeton, & was ordained, & married & installed pastor of the Liberty St. Presb Ch. Troy N.Y. in 1855

In 1859 I lost my wife by whom I had three children, & saw some sorrow about that time. In .59 also I was called to the First Colored Presb. Ch. in Phila. My old home. I grew from infancy in this church & was much attached to the people. I remained with [illegible] taking an active part to sustain the [illegible]nment of the U.S. in the war against Slave Holders Rebellion; & in .64 came [illegible] and opened Missions for the Presb. among the Freedmen in North and

This 1869 letter from Gibbs lists his accomplishments.

Set It!

Jonathan Clarkson Gibbs wanted to be educated. His first step in reaching that goal was to find a church that would help him.

Set a goal that you want to reach. Then, plan how you can reach your goal. What steps will you take to reach that goal? Will you need help from other people? How will you know when you have reached your goal? Share your plan with your friends or family.

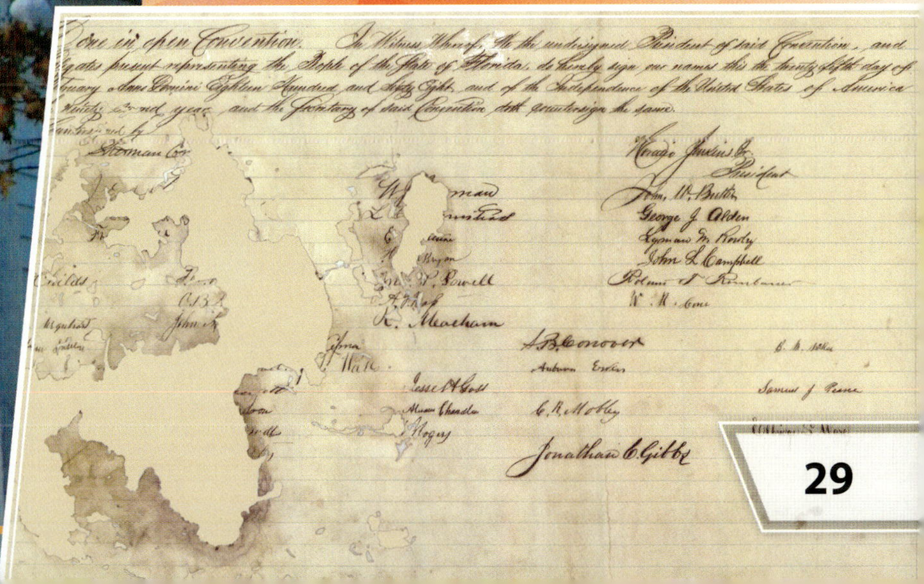

one in open Convention. In Witness Whereof, We the undersigned President of said Convention, and
gates present representing the People of the State of Florida, do hereby sign our names this the twenty fifth day of
ruary Anno Domini Eighteen Hundred and Sixty Eight, and of the Independence of the United States of America
ninety second year, and the Secretary of said Convention doth countersign the same.

Glossary

abolitionist—a person who wants to abolish or stop slavery

apprentice—a person who is taught a job or trade by a skilled worker

charismatic—having great charm that appeals to others

Civil War—the war fought between the Northern and Southern states over the issues of slavery and state rights

freedmen—former slaves who have been freed

ghastly—shocking or horrible

governor—a person who is the leader of a region

impeach—to charge a public official in office with a crime

ordained—officially made a minister or priest

rebels—people from the Southern states who fought against the Union in the Civil War

Reconstruction—the years after the Civil War when the country reformed

secretary of state—U.S. leader who facilitates the country's relations with foreign countries

segregation—the practice of separating groups of people based on their race or religion

seminary—a school that prepares religious leaders, such as ministers

superintendent of public instruction—a government official in charge of education in a state

Underground Railroad—a network of people and safe places that helped runaway slaves reach safety before and during the Civil War

Index

Your Turn!

Political Ad

This political ad from 1866 shows two images. How did the artist depict the person on the left? How did the artist depict the person on the right? Why might the artist have chosen to draw the people in this way? Write about what this ad communicates about the time period.